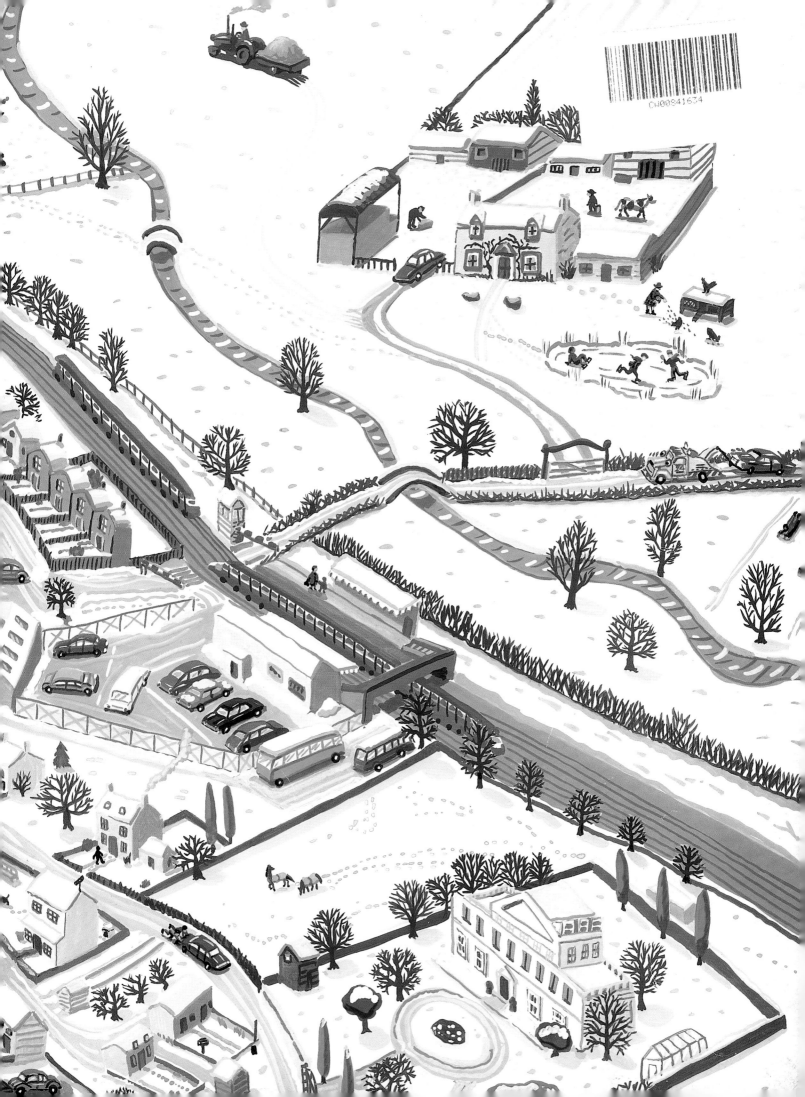

If you meet Jack Tractor
You're sure to get along.
He makes a lovely friend because
He's happy, big and strong!

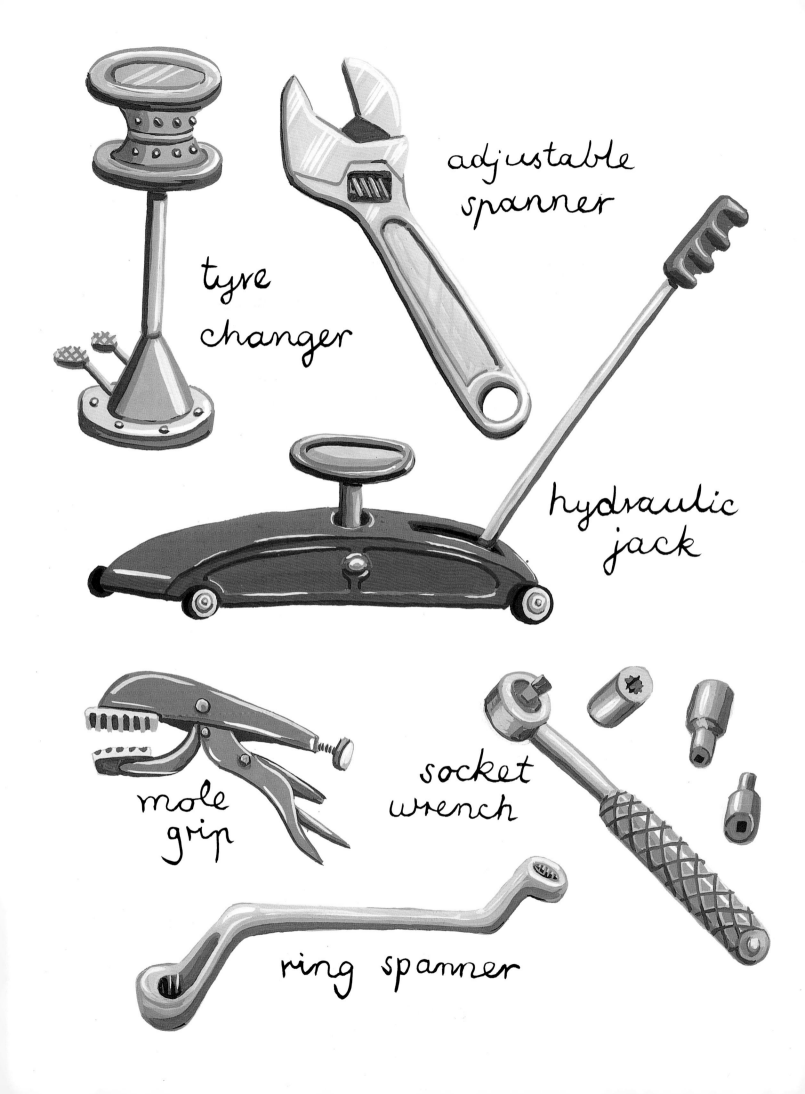

tyre changer

adjustable spanner

hydraulic jack

mole grip

socket wrench

ring spanner

mallet

spanner

Jack Tractor

FIVE STORIES FROM SMALLBILLS GARAGE

Keren Ludlow and Willy Smax

ratchet screwdriver

Orion
Children's Books

for Magnus

First published in Great Britain in 1995
by Orion Children's Books
a division of the Orion Publishing Group Ltd
Orion House
5 Upper St Martin's Lane
London WC2H 9EA

Text copyright © Willy Smax 1995
Illustrations copyright © Keren Ludlow 1995

Willy Smax and Keren Ludlow have asserted
their right to be identified as the author
and illustrator of this work.

CONTENTS

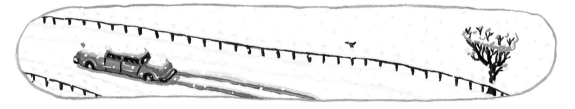

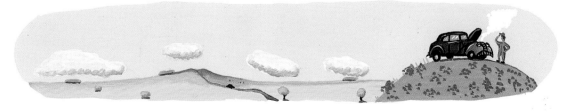

Jack Tractor and the Chicken Coop

It was early morning in Brummingham. Mike McCannick opened the automatic doors at Smallbills Garage.

"Morning, Benny," said Mike. "I've got a tough job for you today. Jack Tractor's stuck in the mud up on Bedstead Farm and you've got to pull him out."

"That sounds like fun," said Benny.

"Wait until you see how deep the mud is," said Mike, pulling on his rubber boots.

"If you hurry up you'll be in time for breakfast with the pigs!" said Francis Ford Popular. Benny ignored him.

Benny and Mike drove out of the garage, down the high street, over the level crossing and out into the country.

As they went over the hill and through the gates to Bedstead Farm they saw poor Jack Tractor standing in the middle of the duck pond, up to his hubcaps in water.

"What happened?" asked Benny.

"My brakes failed as I was coming down the hill," groaned the big red tractor.

Mike fixed Benny's tow-hook to Jack's front axle and Benny began to pull.

Benny pulled hard, but Jack was stuck fast.
Suddenly there was a loud gurgling noise,
and Jack shot forward. So did Benny. BANG!
He crashed into the chicken coop. All the hens
flew up into the air, squawking with fright.

"No damage done," said Farmer Pyjama,
and he put the chicken coop back up again.

Mike dried Jack's spark plugs and topped up his brake fluid. After a few tries Jack's engine started. Farmer Pyjama was so pleased that he invited Mike to the Bedstead Farm barn dance.

"Oh, please may I come too!" said Benny.

"Sorry," said Mike. "You know I always take Francis when I go out in the evenings."

Back at the garage Francis Ford Popular looked at the muddy breakdown truck.

"So you did have breakfast with the pigs !" he said.

Benny was about to reply when SPLOOSH!
Mike hosed water all over his muddy wheels.
There was a loud squawk from under Benny's
engine, and a big brown hen flew up into
the rafters.

"Look at that!" shouted Mike. "She must
have landed on you when you crashed into
the henhouse."

Mike was just about
to climb into Francis
Ford Popular when
the hen laid an egg.
It dropped SPLAT!
on to his windscreen.

"OOOH!" Francis shrieked.

"What a mess," said Mike. "There's no time to clean that up now. I'll have to go in Benny."

"YIPPEE!" cried Benny. "Let's go! Enjoy your supper, Francis," he called as he drove off. "I expect you'll be having scrambled eggs!"

The End

Carmen gets Trapped

One sunny afternoon Benny the Breakdown Truck and Mike McCannick were just leaving Smallbills Garage to pick up some new tyres when Carmen Gear drove past.

"What a lovely car," said Benny dreamily. "I wish I could meet her."

"She wouldn't speak to a mucky truck like you," said Francis Ford Popular. "She's a classic car like me." And he smiled smugly.

"Take no notice of him," said Mike. "Let's go."

Benny and Mike drove off after Carmen.
As they came to the traffic lights, Alfie Romeo
swerved in front of them. Benny had to screech
to a stop.

"What's going on?" said Benny. "You nearly
caused an accident."

"I'm in a hurry and you're in the way," said
Alfie. And he raced off as soon as the lights
changed to green.

He didn't see the huge truck with the
heavy load of logs coming the other way.

23

All the logs rolled off, trapping poor Carmen Gear underneath them.

"Look out!" shouted the truck, swerving across the road to avoid Alfie.

GET ME OUT OF HERE!

shouted Carmen.

Benny leapt into action. He parked next to Carmen Gear and swung his tow-hook around the log. Then he winched as hard as he could until he had lifted all the logs back on to the lorry. Luckily Carmen wasn't hurt.

Alfie saw his chance. "If you're feeling okay, would you like to go for a drive tonight?" he asked Carmen.

"Yes, I'd love to," said Carmen, looking at Benny. "If Benny will go with me."

Alfie was mortified but Benny was so happy he only just manged to say, "Okay."

"Then I'll see you at the garage at six o'clock," said Carmen as she drove off.

At six o'clock Benny was parked outside Smallbills Garage waiting for Carmen.

Mike had waxed his yellow paintwork and it was shining like the sun.

"Just look at you!" said Francis Ford Popular. "You look like a melon."

"And smell like a lemon," said Alfie.

"Shut up, you two," said Mike, "you're only jealous."

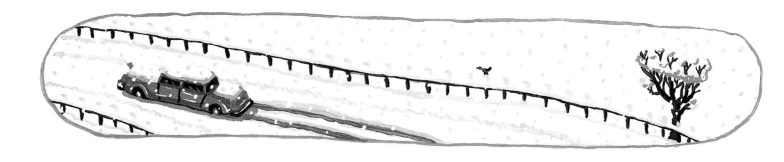

Roland Catches Cold

One winter's morning Mike McCannick came in through the automatic doors to Smallbills Garage and let in an icy blast of cold air.

"Thank goodness you're here!" said Francis Ford Popular. "You can put the stove on. My tyres are freezing."

BEEP!

Mike was just about to light the stove when there was a loud blast from a horn. "BEEP!"

"Who on earth was that?" said Francis irritably.

It was Roland Royce, Brummingham's smartest car. He drove into the garage, his metallic blue paintwork gleaming in the frosty air.

"Oh, it's *you*, Roland," said Francis, suddenly becoming friendly. "How good of you to visit."

"Can't stop," said Roland. "I'm just popping in to have my tyre pressure checked. I've got an important meeting at the airport."

"Terribly cold weather we're having," said Francis, as Mike checked Roland's big wheels with his pressure gauge. "It looks as if it might snow."

"Wouldn't bother me if it did," said Roland. "My engine can cope with anything."

"Why don't you have a drop of anti-freeze?" said Francis. "It's just what you need on a day like this."

"I haven't got time to hang around just for an anti-freeze," boomed Roland Royce grandly, and with a squeal of his tyres he sped off.

Francis was quite upset. "I was only being friendly," he said.

"Roland is always busy," said Benny. "He'll probably stop by for a chat some other time."

"Not in a cold old garage like this one," said Francis, and he stared sadly out of the garage doors as the snow began to fall.

"Poor old Francis," said Mike. "Let's make it nice and warm for you." He stoked up the stove until it was glowing brightly. Outside, the snow began to fall faster and faster, covering the ground with a blanket of white.

Suddenly the phone rang. It was Roland Royce calling from his car phone.

"He's got stuck in the snow," said Mike. "We'll have to go and pull him out, Benny."

Benny couldn't wait to go out in the beautiful white snow. He drove off towards the airport, leaving two long tracks behind him.

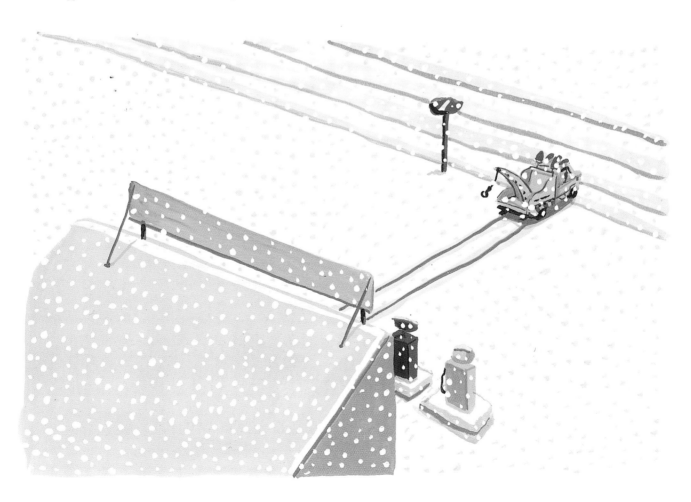

"There's Roland!" he cried. "He's skidded into a drift."

"Thank goodness you've come!" said Roland. "I'm so cold! My engine has completely frozen up. And I've missed my meeting at the airport."

"Don't worry, Roland," said Mike. "I'll just hook you up to Benny's tow bar and we'll be home in no time."

Roland couldn't wait to get inside the warm, cosy garage. Benny towed him right up to the stove to thaw out his engine.

"This would never have happened if I'd stayed for that anti-freeze you offered me," said Roland to Francis.

"That's all right," said Francis. "You can have it now if you like." And the two friends chatted happily by the stove as Mike poured out two large cans of anti-freeze.

"This is much more fun than driving to the airport," said Roland. "What a lovely place you have here."

"Can't complain," said Francis, "can't complain."

Morton at the Building Site

Morton the naughty blue motorbike had spent the whole morning watching the busy building site on the other side of Spanner Street.

He thought the red dumper truck was having the most fun, tipping cement into holes.

Morton was so busy watching that he didn't notice Mike arrive with a large package.

"Morning, Morton," said Mike. "Look what I've got for you."

Mike had bought a big blue and white top box so that Morton could carry his tools when they went out to work together.

"Just what I've always wanted," said Morton, flashing his headlights.

"It's only for carrying tools," said Mike, "so don't go getting into mischief with it."

But Morton couldn't wait to use his brand new top box. As soon as Mike had gone the naughty blue motor bike sneaked off to the building site over the road. He went straight up to the red dumper truck, who was tipping cement into square holes in the ground.

"I bet I could do that," said Morton.

"Oh yeah?" said the dumper truck.

"Just watch me!" said Morton. He rode up to the cement mixer, filled up his brand new top box with a big load of sludgy cement, and carried the cement over to the foundation holes.

"And just how are you going to tip it in, Mister clever bike?" asked the dumper truck.

"Easy peasy," said Morton. "I'll just do a wheelie."

And with a flick of his accelerator his front wheel leapt into the air and the cement tipped neatly out of his top box and into one of the holes.

"You'd better be careful doing that," said the dumper truck. "It's muddy here and you might slip. You wouldn't want to land up stuck in the cement."

"Not me!" said Morton. "Come on, I bet I can fill up more holes than you can!" And he raced off to get some more cement.

As soon as his top box was full he sped back and twisted his throttle to do another wheelie.

But he was going far too fast, and he spun head over wheels in the air. "WHOOO!"

WHOOO!

screamed Morton, as he landed with both wheels stuck in the cement.

"Please get Benny to pull me out," he pleaded.

The red dumper truck could hardly stop sniggering as he drove off to find Benny.

"Hurry up!" shouted Morton, who could already feel the cement drying on his wheels.

It seemed ages before Benny came, and he couldn't help smiling as he swung his tow-hook under Morton.

When Benny lifted Morton out of the holes there were two big blocks of cement set on his wheels. Poor Morton was mortified.

CRASH! went Morton as Benny lowered him on to the garage forecourt. Mike rushed out to see what the noise was about.

"What on earth have you got on your wheels?" shouted Mike.

"Oh, just a bit of cement," said Morton.

"A bit?" said Mike. "You've got half a building there!"

"I know," said Morton sadly. "Do you think you can get it off?"

Mike reached into his toolbox and pulled out the largest hammer and chisel he could find.

"With pleasure!" he said.

Spare Part for Francis

It was a lovely summer's day, and Mike McCannick was out for a drive in the country with Francis Ford Popular.

The old motor car was enjoying himself. He hummed along happily until they came to Bedstead Hill. Halfway up he started to slow down.

"I'm not as new as I used to be," he puffed.

Francis only just made it to the top of the hill. His temperature gauge started to rise and a big cloud of white steam came out from under his bonnet.

"You don't sound too good to me," said Mike as he turned off the engine. "We'd better have a look at you." And they freewheeled down the hill all the way back to Smallbills Garage.

"Oh!" cried Benny as Francis rolled silently through the door. "You did give me a shock, creeping up on me like that!"

"Well, you won't have to put up with me upsetting you like that for much longer," said Francis in a shaky voice. "You'll be towing me to the scrapyard soon."

"Stop moaning," said Mike, opening his toolbox. "You've probably blown a gasket. I'll have it fixed in no time."

He crawled under Francis's engine. After a while he came out with his hands all black and oily.

"It's much worse than I thought," he said. "I'm afraid your crankshaft has gone. I'd better phone round the car spares shops and see if I can find a replacement."

He tried number after number, but no one had a crankshaft for such an old car.

"Oh, don't bother," said Francis, his headlamps looking dim. "Just tow me to the scrapyard. It will save a lot of fuss."

"That's a thought," said Benny, starting up his engine, and he began to drive out of the garage.

"That's right," said Francis. "You go off and enjoy yourself. Just leave me here to rust in peace."

But Benny had had an idea.

He drove straight to the Brummingham
scrapyard and spoke to Ivan the forklift truck.

"You wouldn't happen to have a spare crankshaft for a Ford Popular, would you?" said Benny.

"Might do," said Ivan Forklift. He went to look, while Benny crossed his windscreen wipers and waited.

Before long Ivan came back with a gleaming crankshaft on his forks.

"I think this is what you're looking for," said Ivan, lowering the crankshaft over Benny's tailgate.

"Thanks, Ivan!" said Benny. "Must dash!" And he raced back to Smallbills Garage.

When he came through the door, Mike and Francis were looking very sad indeed.

"I couldn't find one anywhere," said Mike unhappily.

"At least you tried," said Francis, "not like *some* vehicles I could mention who just go out enjoying themselves."

"I haven't been out enjoying myself," said Benny. "I've been to the scrapyard."

"Well," said Francis, "did they have any room for me?"

"No," said Benny, swinging his crane around, "but they did have this!"

Francis could hardly believe his headlamps. There was a shiny crankshaft hanging from Benny's tow-hook.

"Well done, Benny," said Mike. "Bring it over and I'll put it in."

Mike worked all night replacing the broken crankshaft, and the next day Francis was ready for a test drive.

"It's another beautiful day," said Mike. "Let's go back to Bedstead Hill."

The three friends raced up the hill together.

"Well," said Mike, "you're sounding a lot better now."

"I certainly am," said Francis, beaming. "Thanks to Benny!"

The End

If you've just been to Brummingham
And now you're going back,
Why not stop at Bedstead Farm
And say hello to Jack!